YOU SEE A CIRCUS.
I SEE . . .

Mike Downs

Illustrated by Anik McGrory

Charlesbridge

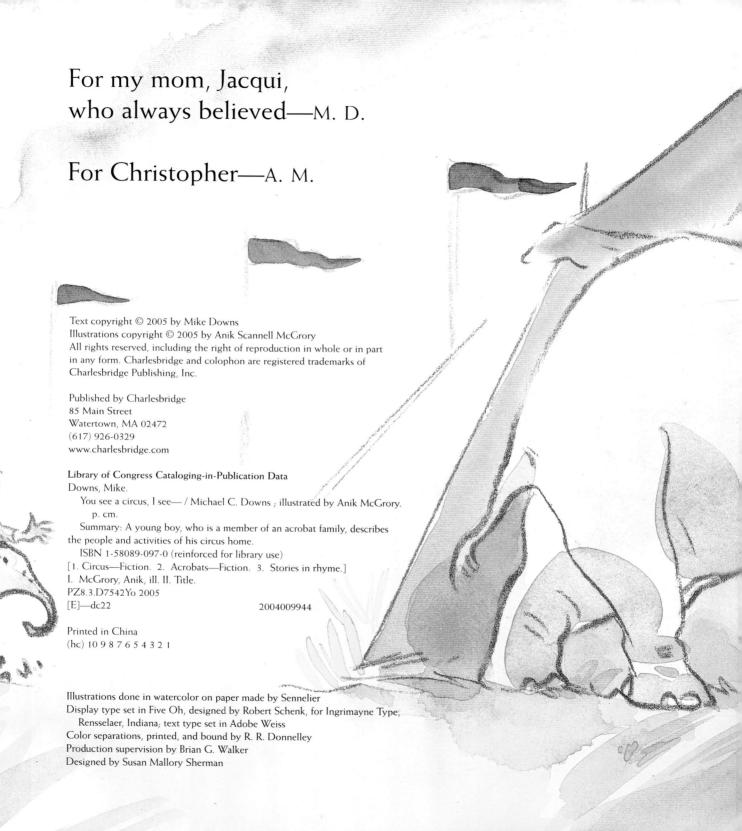

For my mom, Jacqui,
who always believed—M. D.

For Christopher—A. M.

Text copyright © 2005 by Mike Downs
Illustrations copyright © 2005 by Anik Scannell McGrory

Published by Charlesbridge
85 Main Street
Watertown, MA 02472
(617) 926-0329
www.charlesbridge.com

Library of Congress Cataloging-in-Publication Data
Downs, Mike.
  You see a circus, I see— / Michael C. Downs ; illustrated by Anik McGrory.
    p. cm.
  Summary: A young boy, who is a member of an acrobat family, describes
the people and activities of his circus home.
  ISBN 1-58089-097-0 (reinforced for library use)
[1. Circus—Fiction. 2. Acrobats—Fiction. 3. Stories in rhyme.]
I. McGrory, Anik, ill. II. Title.
PZ8.3.D7542Yo 2005
[E]—dc22   2004009944

Printed in China
(hc) 10 9 8 7 6 5 4 3 2 1

Illustrations done in watercolor on paper made by Sennelier
Display type set in Five Oh, designed by Robert Schenk, for Ingrimayne Type,
    Rensselaer, Indiana; text type set in Adobe Weiss
Color separations, printed, and bound by R. R. Donnelley
Production supervision by Brian G. Walker
Designed by Susan Mallory Sherman

The circus is here! It's come to town.
Lions, acrobats, elephants, clowns.
Kids of all ages rush to get in;
The world's greatest show is about to begin.

You see a strong man.

Solid as stone, strong as a bear,
Muscles bulging everywhere,
This amazing giant man
Bends an iron rod by hand.

I see my uncle.

He picks me up with just one arm
And tells me I'm his lucky charm.
We wrestle every chance we get.
It's strange; he's never pinned me yet.

You see a lion tamer.

He takes his place, center stage
With wild lions in a cage.
Some people think that he's a fool
To face six lions with a stool.

I see my teacher.

He tutors me in math and art;
In fact, he really is quite smart.
But he's not fearless, as it seems:
When I surprise him, he sure screams.

You see a juggler.

She grabs a broom and ball and chair;
Then tosses them into the air.
She performs this wondrous feat
Atop a unicycle seat.

I see my best friend.

In the circus train we ride,
We live in rail cars, side by side.
Together we play cards or chess
And share our dreams of great success.

You see a tattooed man.

With skulls and serpents head to toe,
His tattoos even seem to glow.
He's fearsome-looking, very grim;
You'd never stay alone with him!

I see silly Joe.

He fools around with goofy things,
From beanie hats to squirting rings.
And he can really play a joke,
Like when he makes his sneakers smoke.

You see trapeze artists.

Two acrobats in snazzy tights
Soar overhead while chased by lights.
From platforms high above the ground,
They leap . . . then flip and spin around.

I see my parents.

My mom and dad are really neat;
To see them fly is quite a treat.
But when we're off to have some fun,
They still make sure my homework's done.

You see a clown.

He wears enormous spotted ties
And rides a trike while dodging pies.
His silly stunts make people laugh,
And kids sure love his autograph.

I see quiet Mike.

He's really funny in the show,
But afterward he'll always go
And find himself a peaceful nook
Where he can sit and read a book.

You see a boy on a horse.

He spins and twirls double-quick
To carry out this saddle trick.
Next he swings from side to side,
Then stands and waves to end his ride!

I see me.

It's fun to be an acrobat,
But I work hard to do my act.
I have to practice hours each day
To ride my horse this special way.

You see a circus.

Tattooed men, trapeze stars,
Mighty strong men bending bars.
Jugglers, clowns, acrobats,
Lion tamers, roaring cats.
All beneath a three-ringed dome.

But when I see a circus,

I see . . .
Home!